DAMON, PYTHIAS,
and the Test of Friendship

Retold by **Teresa Bateman**

Paintings by **Layne Johnson**

Albert Whitman & Company, Morton Grove, Illinois

For Joshua, who has already taught us much
about faith and courage.—T.B.

To Brett—I'm proud you're my son and
also one of my best friends.—L.J.

Library of Congress Cataloging-in-Publication Data

Bateman, Teresa.
Damon, Pythias, and the test of friendship / retold by Teresa Bateman ;
paintings by Layne Johnson.
p. cm.
ISBN 978-0-8075-1445-0
1. Damon (Greek mythology)—Juvenile literature.
2. Phintias (Greek mythology)—Juvenile literature.
I. Johnson, Layne. II. Title.
BL820.D28B38 2009   398.20938′02—dc22   2008034559

Text copyright © 2009 by Teresa Bateman.
Illustrations copyright © 2009 by Layne Johnson.
Published in 2009 by Albert Whitman & Company,
6340 Oakton Street, Morton Grove, Illinois 60053-2723.
Published simultaneously in Canada by Fitzhenry & Whiteside,
Markham, Ontario. All rights reserved. No part of this book
may be reproduced or transmitted in any form or by any means,
electronic or mechanical, including photocopying, recording, or
by any information storage and retrieval system, without
permission in writing from the publisher.
Printed in China.
10 9 8 7 6 5 4 3 2 1

The design is by Carol Gildar.

For more information about Albert Whitman & Company,
please visit our web site at www.albertwhitman.com.

The names in this story are from the Greek language.
Their pronunciations are: Damon (DAY muhn); Pythias (PIHTH ee uhs);
and Dionysius (Dy uh NIHSH ee us).

ITALY

Tyrrhenian Sea

Ionian Sea

SICILY

•Syracuse

Long ago in Sicily, there lived a cruel ruler named Dionysius. He believed in friendship no more than he believed in mermaids or dragons. "A friend?" Dionysius said. "A friend is only someone who will trick you into trusting him and then betray that trust."

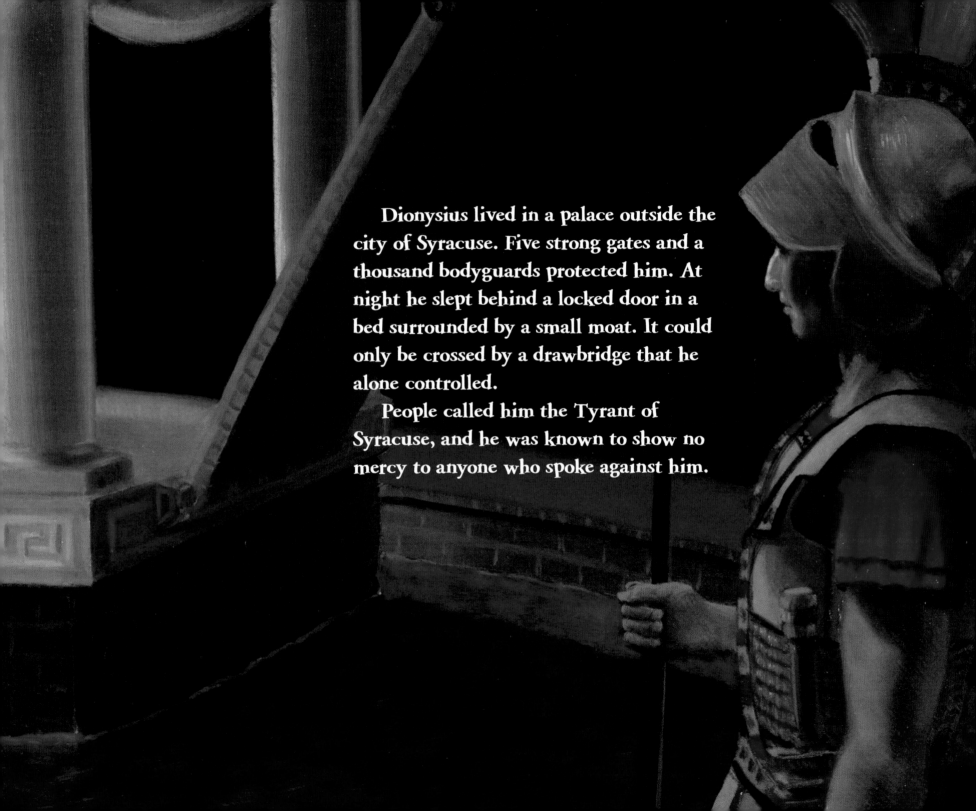

Dionysius lived in a palace outside the city of Syracuse. Five strong gates and a thousand bodyguards protected him. At night he slept behind a locked door in a bed surrounded by a small moat. It could only be crossed by a drawbridge that he alone controlled.

People called him the Tyrant of Syracuse, and he was known to show no mercy to anyone who spoke against him.

Dionysius did not believe in friendship, but in Syracuse there lived two young men who did. Their names were Damon and Pythias. They were best friends and shared nearly everything, including doubts about their ruler.

One day Pythias gave a speech in the marketplace. He spoke against Dionysius, saying he was a bad ruler.

Suddenly the bodyguards of Dionysius appeared. "Run!" people shouted. "Hide!" But it was already too late. The soldiers marched Pythias off to their master to be sentenced for treason.

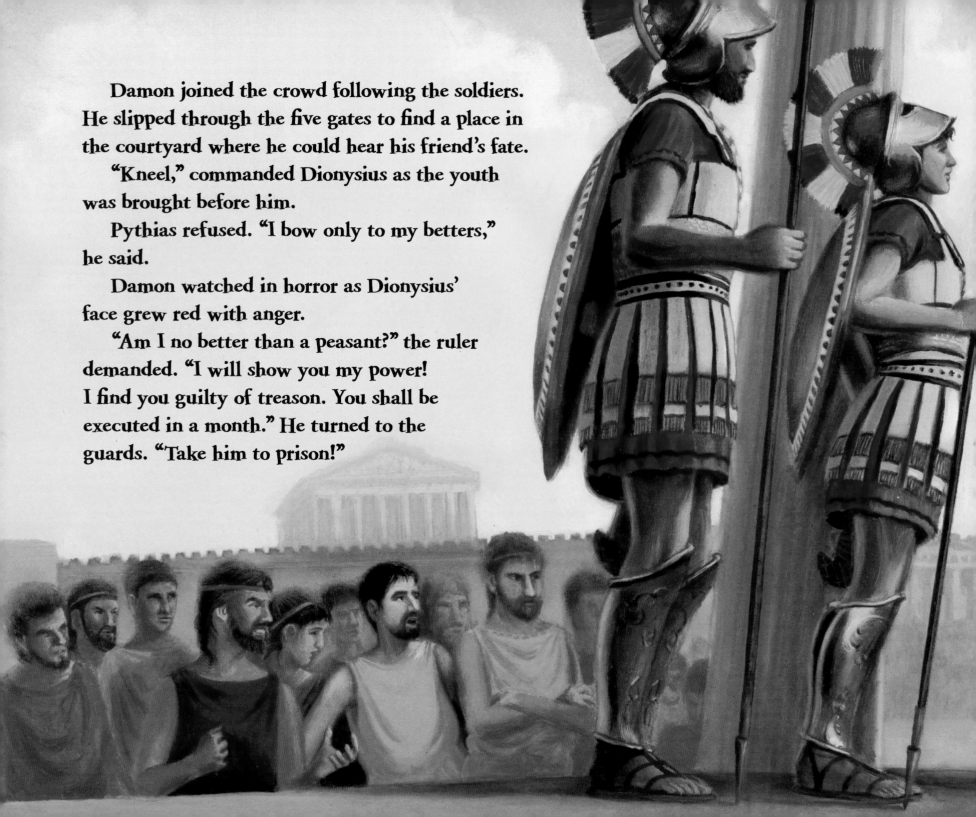

Damon joined the crowd following the soldiers.
He slipped through the five gates to find a place in
the courtyard where he could hear his friend's fate.

"Kneel," commanded Dionysius as the youth
was brought before him.

Pythias refused. "I bow only to my betters,"
he said.

Damon watched in horror as Dionysius'
face grew red with anger.

"Am I no better than a peasant?" the ruler
demanded. "I will show you my power!
I find you guilty of treason. You shall be
executed in a month." He turned to the
guards. "Take him to prison!"

Pythias, pale as ashes, stood his ground. "If I must, I will die for my beliefs," he said. "But I ask one favor. My parents are old. Let me go home to say farewell and arrange for their care. I will return in a month for my punishment."

Dionysius laughed. "Let you go? You would never come back, knowing that death waits for you."

"I give you my word I will return," Pythias vowed.

"Your word means nothing to me," Dionysius declared.

Then, to the crowd's astonishment, Damon stepped forward. "Pythias is my friend. Let me take his place in prison until he returns."

"And if he does not return?" Dionysius questioned.

"Then I will die in his stead," said Damon.

The Tyrant of Syracuse was puzzled, sure some trick was involved. "Very well," he finally agreed. "But if Pythias does not return, I will not spare you from punishment. One of you shall die."

Pythias turned to his friend. "I will come back as quickly as I can. Trust in me."

"I always have," Damon replied.

So Damon was taken to prison in his friend's place.

People in Syracuse wondered if the young men's friendship would be strong enough for such a test.

In the prison, the other men laughed at Damon. "You were a fool to trust Pythias," they said.

But Damon's faith remained unshaken.

Each day, Dionysius
visited Damon's cell.
"Where is your friend?"
he would ask.

"Pythias will return,"
Damon would always reply.
"I am sure of it."

Yet time was passing,
and the month was nearly
gone.

Pythias traveled quickly and soon reached his home. When he told his parents what had happened, they wept. They pleaded with him to forget his promise and stay with them, but he refused.

"My friend trusts me," he told them simply. "I am here only to say goodbye and to make arrangements for your future."

His business took longer than he had planned.
Finally Pythias started the long journey back to
Syracuse. If he hurried, he could arrive within
the promised month.

Perhaps because he was
hurrying, he didn't notice the
robbers until it was too late.
They took his money and left
him battered and unconscious
beside the road.

Execution day arrived, but Pythias did not. People shook their heads. Who could keep such a pledge? Yet their hearts sank at the price to be paid.

The prisoner was brought before the Tyrant of Syracuse for execution.

"So," taunted Dionysius. "Now you see the folly of trusting others. Do you still believe in Pythias?"

"I do," Damon replied. "He would be here if he could. I will gladly give my life for that of my friend."

Dionysius seemed to hesitate. Then he shouted angrily, "Summon the executioner!"

Damon knelt before Dionysius.

Suddenly there was a disturbance outside the courtyard.
Through the gates ran a ragged, travel-worn figure who
staggered forward, threw himself down beside Damon, and
embraced him, weeping.

"I am in time! Thank the gods I am in time!"

Pythias had come.

"I knew you would return," Damon said. "I never doubted."

Pythias turned to Dionysius. "I am ready to receive my punishment," he said. "Free my friend."

"No! I would gladly die that you might live," Damon said.

Back and forth went the argument, for neither wished to live at the price of the other's death.

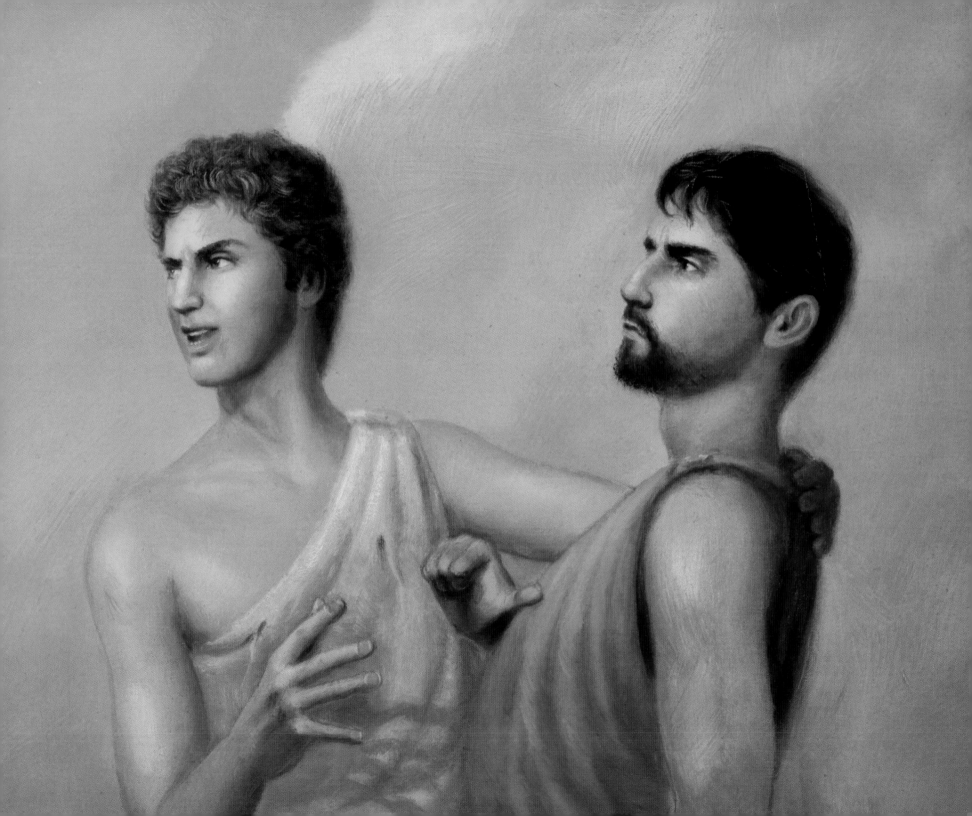

"Stop this arguing!" shouted the Tyrant of Syracuse.

There was a long silence. Dionysius had a strange look on his face, like that of a thirsty man seeing water after a desert journey.

"I revoke the sentence of death," he said at last. "You are both free to go. But could you grant me one favor?"

Damon and Pythias stood shoulder to shoulder, facing their ruler.

Dionysius spoke humbly, "Might I be the third in your friendship?"

Note

The tale of Damon and Pythias takes place in the fourth century B.C.E. on the island of Sicily in the Mediterranean Sea. The events of the story are believed to have really happened. Several ancient writers have retold the story, including a man called Valerius Maximus who recorded it in his book *De Amicitiae Vinculo [On the Chains of Friendship]*, which was published in 25 C.E.

We know Dionysius I was a real person. He was born about 430 B.C.E. and died in 367 B.C.E. He was a ruthless Greek warrior who rose to become supreme military commander of Syracuse in 406 B.C.E. The next year, he proclaimed himself ruler of Syracuse, which is on the island of Sicily. He was a dangerous man, and everyone knew it.

Such a ruler would naturally have enemies, and Dionysius always feared for his own safety, never trusting those around him. A famous example of this is found in another story. A man named Damocles told Dionysius how much he admired his spacious home, his large army, and his many possessions. He was sure Dionysius must be the happiest man on earth.

Dionysius offered to let Damocles taste the life of a wealthy man. Damocles slept in a golden bed and was pampered by a crowd of servants. When he was led to the table, he found it filled with the richest foods. But after he was seated, Damocles looked up and discovered that over his head was a sword, hung from the rafters by a single horsehair thread. Any moment the sword might fall. Suddenly all the wealth became meaningless, and he asked to resume his normal life. Dionysius laughed and explained that the wealth and power that Damocles admired came with a price. Due to those who hated and envied him, Dionysius' life often hung by a thread.

Most people today have never heard of Dionysius. However, though well over two thousand years have passed, the story of Damon and Pythias endures as an example of brotherly love and true friendship.